CARDIFF EMPIRE
QUEEN STREET

PROPRIETORS .... MOSS EMPIRES, LIMITED.
Managing Director .... Mr. FRANK ALLEN.
Acting Manager .... HERBERT J. TAYLOR.

MONDAY, JAN. 6th, 1913 and TWICE NIGHTLY
AT 6.45 AND 9.0 DURING THE WEEK.

THE WORLD-FAMOUS SELF-LIBERATOR !

HOUDINI

Presenting the Greatest Performance of his Strenuous Career, liberating himself after being Locked in a

WATER TORTURE CELL

Houdini's own Invention, whilst Standing on his Head his Ankles Clamped and Locked above in the Centre of the Massive Cover. A Feat which borders on to the Supernatural.

£200 Houdini offers this sum to anyone proving that it is possible to obtain air in the upside-down position in which he releases himself from this WATER-FILLED TORTURE CELL.

CASELLI SISTERS
Vocalists and Dancers

HAPPY TOM PARKER
COMEDIAN AND DANCER

For my parents

—◈—

and with special thanks
to Steve Geck and Diana Blough

Atheneum Books for Young Readers
An imprint of Simon & Schuster Children's Publishing Division
1230 Avenue of the Americas, New York, New York 10020
The poster "Harry Houdini: King of Cards" originally appeared in Milbourne
Christopher's *Houdini: A Pictorial Life* (New York, 1976) and is used here
by the kind permission of Mrs. Maurine Christopher.
The photograph of Harry Houdini pulling a rabbit from his hat originally appeared
in Walter B. Gibson's *The Original Houdini Scrapbook* and is used here
by the kind permission of Robert W. Gibson.
The photograph of Houdini in chains courtesy of the
Library of Congress, LC-USZC4-3277.
Houdini's portrait courtesy of the Library of Congress, LC-USZ62-112431.
The text for this book is set in Old Style 7.
The illustrations for this book are rendered in pen.
Manufactured in the United States of America
0110 WOR
4 6 8 10 9 7 5 3
CIP data for this book is available from the Library of Congress.
ISBN-13: 978-1-4169-6878-8
ISBN-10: 1-4169-6878-4

THE
HOUDINI
BOX

Written and illustrated by
BRIAN SELZNICK

Atheneum Books for Young Readers

New York   London   Toronto   Sydney

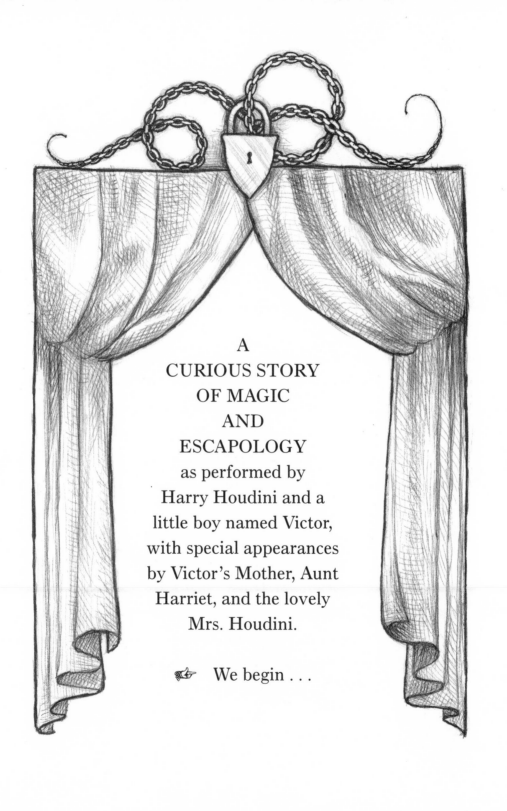

A
CURIOUS STORY
OF MAGIC
AND
ESCAPOLOGY
as performed by
Harry Houdini and a
little boy named Victor,
with special appearances
by Victor's Mother, Aunt
Harriet, and the lovely
Mrs. Houdini.

☞   We begin . . .

OUDINI was a magician. He could pull rabbits from hats, make elephants disappear, and do a thousand card tricks. Locks would fall open at his fingertips, and he could escape from ropes and chains and cabinets and coffins. Police from around the world couldn't keep him in their jails, and the oceans and the seas couldn't drown him. Bolt Houdini into a metal box and throw him in the water; he will escape. Lock him up in a jail, hand-cuffed and helpless, in any city in the world—Moscow, New York, Vienna, Paris, or Providence; Houdini will escape.

Everyone was wonderstruck by Houdini, but children were especially delighted. Children ,want to be able to escape their rooms when they are sent there for being bad. They want to make their dinners disappear and their parents vanish. They want to pull candy from their pockets without putting any in, turn their sisters into puppies and their brothers into frogs (although some children want to turn their puppies and frogs into sisters and brothers). Children liked Houdini because he could do the unexplainable things that they wanted to do. Houdini was a magician. Magicians can do anything.

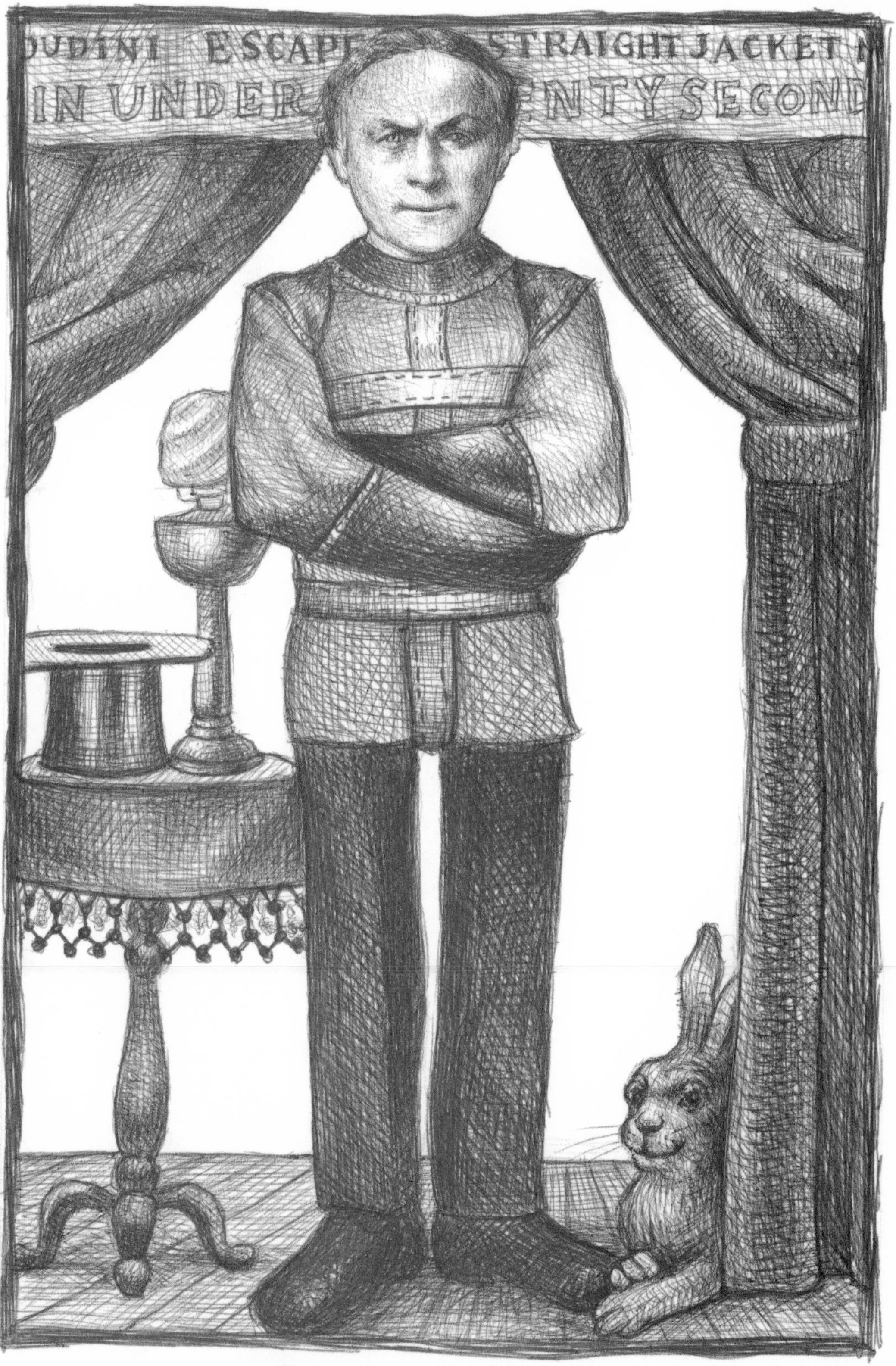
UDINI ESCAPE STRAIGHT JACKET
IN UNDER ENTY SECOND

Victor was ten. He wanted to be a magician too.

When Victor was eight, he read in the newspaper that Houdini had escaped from an iron milk can in under twenty seconds.

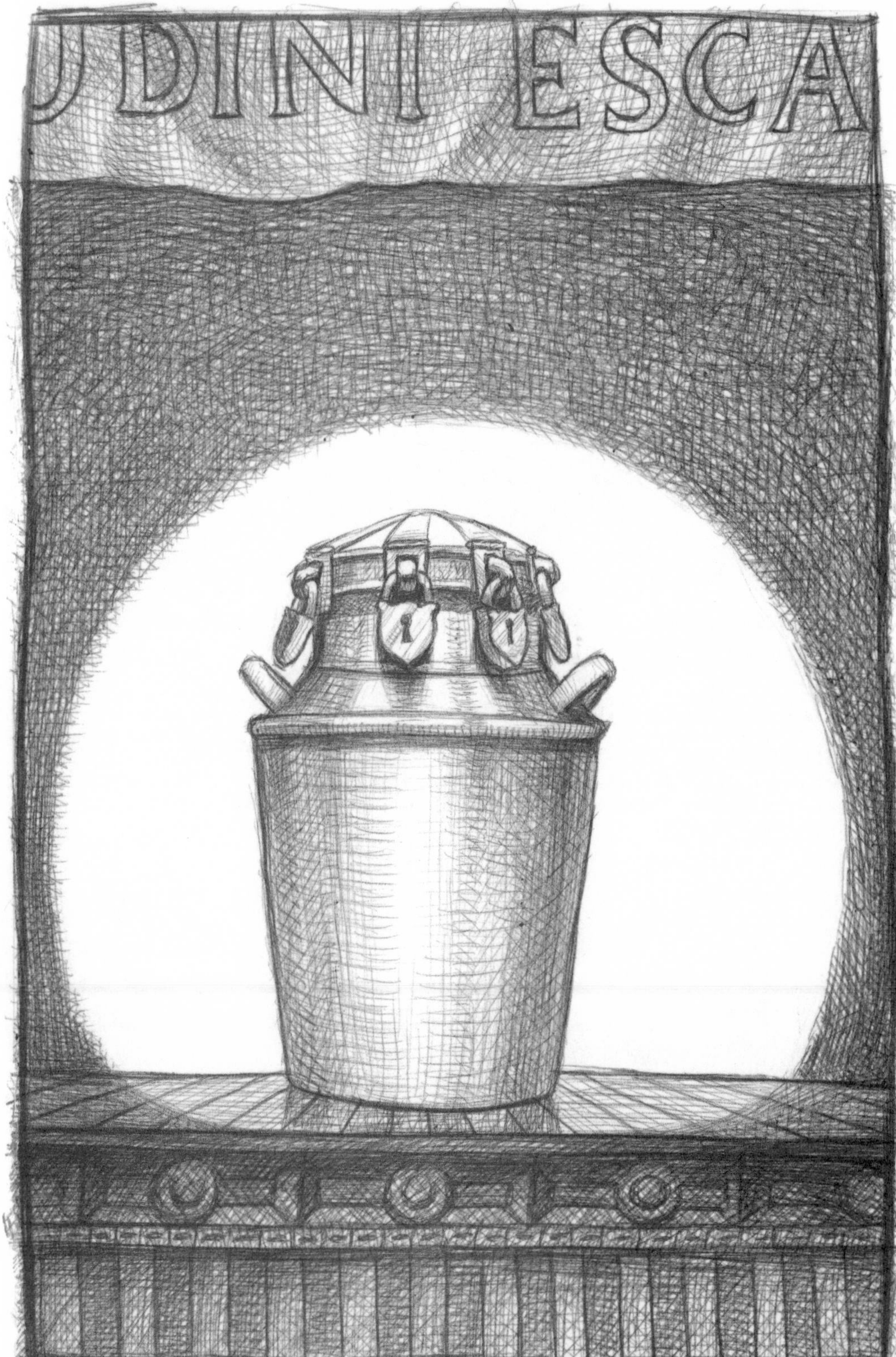
DINI ESCA

Victor found his grandmother's trunk and closed himself inside. The locks snapped shut behind him. He tried and tried, but he could not escape in under twenty seconds. In fact, he could not escape at all.

So Victor cried and yelled until his mother came home and undid the locks. She was very upset that her son had shut himself in Grandmother's trunk. Victor was very upset that he couldn't get out.

When Victor was nine, he found out that Houdini could hold his breath for over five thousand seconds while escaping from a crate dropped into the ocean. If Houdini could hold his breath for five thousand seconds in his crate in the ocean, then Victor could certainly hold his breath for five thousand seconds in his tub in the bathroom. So during bath time, he put his head underwater and counted as fast as he could. But he never got to five thousand. His mother kept making him get out of the tub and breathe.

Victor got this idea when he read that Houdini could walk through brick walls. Victor was sure he could do that. First, he tried walking slowly into a living room wall and pushing his way through. Nothing happened. Next he tried backing up across the room and running through the wall. He almost broke the lamp, the table, a few pictures, and his nose—but he didn't make it to the other side. Later that evening, after many unsuccessful hours, Victor finally got through the wall. He used the door.

Victor's mother was going crazy unlocking her son from trunks, reminding him to breathe when he took a bath, and telling him not to walk into walls. She decided she would take him to visit Aunt Harriet. Maybe a weekend in the country would calm him down.

It was while they were traveling there that the most incredible thing happened.

Victor was looking around the huge, bustling train station when he saw, way across the crowds, Harry Houdini himself, buying tickets with his wife.

Victor broke free from his mother's hand and ran straight to Houdini. He was filled with questions, millions and billions of questions, but which should he ask first? He took a deep breath, and this is what he said:

"How can I escape from my grandmother's trunk in under twenty seconds? How do I hold my breath in the tub without running out of air? Why can't I walk through a wall, like you can? How do you escape from jails and handcuffs and ropes and make elephants disappear? How—"

"Congratulations, my young man," interrupted the smiling magician. "No one has ever asked me so many questions in such a short amount of time. Are you a magician?"

"I want to be one," Victor said.

Houdini remained silent for several moments. After looking at Victor, and then at his wife, he finally said, "Then listen. Give me the tag from your suitcase."

"Why?"

"Your name and address are on it. When I write you a letter, I'll need to know where to send it, won't I?"

Victor immediately undid the little buckle and handed the tag to Houdini.

After reading it, the magician bent down so he was face to face with the boy. He whispered, "You want me to tell you things I can't talk about in the middle of a busy train station, son. And if I'm not mistaken, I see your mother heading this way. If it looks like you're going to get in trouble, you can blame everything on me." Then, grinning ever so slightly, he added, "Tell her Houdini tied you up for a moment. I'll write you a letter. Wait. Just you wait."

Houdini slipped the nametag into his pocket and disappeared into the crowd with his wife.

The weekend in the country was not as restful as Victor's mother had hoped. Her son was so excited about having seen Houdini that he locked himself in Aunt Harriet's dresser and in the cabinet of her clock. He walked very fast into her walls and almost broke all of her old framed photographs. Aunt Harriet was not sad when they left.

Back at home, Victor locked himself in the closet under the staircase, the cupboard in the kitchen, and his grandmother's trunk, nine more times. How he hoped Houdini would write him quickly!

Victor thought and dreamt about the magician's letter. When you are a boy expecting the secrets of the world to arrive in the mail, it is almost impossible to be patient. If only Victor were already a magician! A magician could make the letter appear out of thin air. But Victor was still just a boy, and patiently or not, he had to wait. And so he did, until one day when he was locked up tight inside an old suitcase, he finally heard his mother say, "Victor, there's a letter here for you."

She unlocked the suitcase and handed him the letter.
The handwriting was thick and round and perfect:

*A thousand secrets await you.
Come to my house...*

Then Houdini gave the time and date for the meeting.
But it seemed so far away! Victor knew he couldn't
wait so he went to the magician's house that evening.

His hands were shaking as he knocked on the door. With a heavy sigh it opened, and there before him was Harry Houdini's wife. Victor was suddenly too nervous to speak. He stood silently, staring at the sad woman in the light of the doorway.

She handed him some candy and softly asked, "What are you supposed to be?"

Victor didn't understand what she meant until he saw a ghost, a cowboy, and two little goblins running down the street. In all of his excitement, he had forgotten that tonight was Halloween!

And now he knew what he was supposed to be. "I'm a magician!" he said, and handed Mrs. Houdini the letter.

Mrs. Houdini read it and began to cry. She asked him to please wait inside, and vanished up the staircase into the magician's library, a dark place alive with books and dust and magical things. He held his breath, waiting for Houdini to greet him with outstretched arms and lead him back into that mysterious room.

When someone finally appeared in the hallway, though, it was only Mrs. Houdini again, alone. She came to Victor and handed him a small locked box. Then she opened the front door, and as she showed him out, he heard her whisper, "Houdini died today."

The magician's wife closed the door and left Victor alone with the box. "Bye," he said to the door, and went out, into the streets, toward home.

That night, while he was trying to open the lock on the box with pins and pens and all the small keys from the suitcases and clocks around the house, Victor found the owner's initials engraved on the bottom:

E. W.

This wasn't Houdini's box at all! The owner was some E. W. There could be no secrets in here.

Imagine, as you read this, how it would feel if you had one dream, one hope, one mysterious wish, and then saw it disappear into thin air. That's how Victor felt, and that's why he did what he did next. He took the box that belonged to E. W. and buried it forever at the bottom of his closet. As he closed the door, he made this promise: "Houdini is gone. I will never think about him again or try to do any of his tricks. Cross my heart and hope to die."

So VICTOR grew up and got married. He and his wife had a child, and they named him Harry (in honor of Aunt Harriet, who had passed away one October long ago; he was not named in honor of a certain magician, because Victor said he never, not even once, thought about Houdini).

One chilly day, several years later, Victor and Harry were playing ball in a large field near a graveyard behind their house. Victor was pitching and Harry was swinging his bat, but he could never quite hit the ball. It was nearing dark, and there was time for just one more try. Victor gave Harry a few last-minute batting tips, and then, with all the gentle power that he had, threw the day's final pitch to his son.

Harry closed his eyes, and at exactly the right moment, he swung his bat. He heard a loud crash, opened his eyes, and was amazed to see the ball fly through the sky and land somewhere in the middle of the graveyard.

Victor congratulated his son, and together they climbed over the iron fence to look for the winning baseball. At last they found it, lying in the corner of a dark monument. Whether it had landed there by chance, or by some strange, powerful magic, no one will ever know. But the ball that Victor's son had hit so perfectly had come to rest right on the grave of Houdini!

Victor read the monument. Two smaller words appeared directly below "Houdini," and Victor said them over and over again, because they seemed so familiar. It wasn't until he traced the first letters with his fingers that he understood what he was reading. This was Houdini's real name.

Before he became Houdini, the magician had been a boy named Ehrich Weiss. E. W.!

Victor's head spun, and he laughed out loud. Carrying his son, he ran out of the graveyard, through the baseball field, and into his house.

He was out of breath and crazy with excitement, but he couldn't tell his wife or son what was going on. He waited until they were fast asleep, and then he snuck upstairs into the attic.

Victor found the forgotten box in a moonlit corner under a steady leak in the roof. He carefully picked it up and dried it off. His hand brushed across the lock, and it suddenly crumbled. The water had rusted through the tiny thing completely. How easy it would be to open the box now!

And that night, while his wife and son slept down-
stairs and the attic shadows vanished in the pale, blue
fall of moonlight, Victor locked himself inside his
grandmother's trunk and escaped

in under twenty seconds.

HARRY PULL A HOUDINI?

★ ★ ★ ★ ★ ★ ★

Magician's 'box' still being sought

By PETER M. GIANOTTI

Harry Houdini may have taken his bag of tricks with him.

The magician, who was born in 1874, reportedly said that on the 100th anniversary of the event "a box containing (his) cherished secrets" would be made public by a lawyer.

The birthday party's over and Harry's box is still part of a long disappearing act. The attorney, according to one report, was V. L. Ernst, who was long since gone the way of all illusionists. He departed this life in 1938.

The box's existence—or non-existence —is surely a crisis in the world of presti-digitation. So much so that Ringling Bros. and Barnum & Bailey Circus has initiated a "world-wide search" for it.

* * *

HOUDINI IS BURIED in Glendale's Machpelah Cemetery. The illusionist, whose name was Erich Weiss, died in 1926. Whether he rests at Machpelah is not a clsoed issue. There have been rumblings questioning his real whereabouts, since annual pilgrimages to the gravesite by magic folk have not produced any visible resurrection.

Circus president Irving Feld asks that persons with "the slightest lead" to the location of the box contact him at 62 W. 45 St., in New York, or P.O. Box 2006 in Haines City, Fla.

There is no reward.

And as Mr. Barnum himself once said . . .

The late Harry Houdini, master magician

Queensboro lane closed

The Manhattan-bound outer lane of the lower level of the Queensboro Bridge will be closed for about three months to allow work crews from Consolidated Edison to perform emergency maintenance work, the city's Traffic Department has announced.

AN INTERESTING NOTE

This is a work of fiction, or at least I thought it was when I first wrote the book.

In 1990, while I was researching Houdini's life for this story, I came across an article dated 1974, with the headline "Magician's 'Box' Still Being Sought." It went on to say that Houdini, "who was born in 1874, reportedly said that on the hundredth anniversary of the event, 'a box containing (his) cherished secrets' would be made public . . ." The article also said that the box had not yet been found.

This statement, I believe, is still true.

A BRIEF BIOGRAPHY
OF HOUDINI

The greatest magician of all time really was named Ehrich Weiss. But in reading the autobiography of Jean Eugène Robert-Houdin, a haunting French magician, Ehrich found a hero—and a new name. He added an *I* to the end of "Houdin," thinking the name would then mean "like that person," and the seventeen-year-old boy became Harry Houdini.

Born on March 24, 1874, in Budapest, Hungary, Ehrich was the fifth son of a poor rabbi. The family came to the United States soon after Ehrich's birth, eventually settling in New York City. His mother said he never cried as a baby, and as a child he was a natural athlete. He was introduced to magic by a friend, and they practiced small conjuring tricks with cards and coins. But the secrets of rope escapes fascinated Ehrich the most.

With his new name, Houdini joined his brother Theo in a small magic act. They called themselves the Houdini Brothers. This all changed in 1894 when Harry married Beatrice Rahner, a young showgirl who eventually replaced Theo in the act. Beatrice became Harry's assistant, and they toured Europe in a show filled with magnificent escapes and mysteries. Audiences screamed and fainted and cheered. The Houdinis returned to America, triumphant.

Some of Houdini's most famous magic acts included making an elephant disappear onstage and walking through a brick wall that was constructed right before the audience's eyes. But, of course, it was his escapes that made him the most famous. Arriving in a new town, he would challenge the chief of police to lock him up in their most secure jail, and once he had escaped, all the papers would write about him. He would sometimes have himself tied up in a straitjacket and dangled upside down over a river, and sometimes he'd be locked up tight into a trunk and thrown *into* the river.

Houdini always escaped. Once, onstage, he had himself sealed inside a giant envelope, which he escaped from without ripping, and another time, Harry had himself sewn inside the body of a gigantic sea creature that had washed up on a nearby beach. Harry loved the challenge of being imprisoned inside strange and unique things, so his act was constantly changing and transforming. Sometimes, though, things didn't go exactly as he planned. For example, with the sea monster, the fumes from the formaldehyde preserving the creature almost knocked him unconscious, but he escaped without ripping the stitches that held him in. Audiences would sit for what seemed like hours as Houdini struggled to escape from a straitjacket or handcuffs, but it was never boring. There were times when audiences thought Houdini was really going to die, and when he didn't, it was as if he had escaped from death. The audiences believed *his* sweat was *their* sweat. He was escaping for *them*! Houdini reminded people that anything was possible.

Even when Houdini was not performing, the magician was

constantly busy. He wrote books, starred in fantastic movies, flew the first plane in Australia, and visited famous magicians' graves. He was obsessed with death, and he and his wife promised that the first to die would try to contact the other from the afterlife. In fact, Houdini also became famous during his lifetime for exposing fake spiritualists.

Spiritualists were people who said that they could talk with the dead during a séance, which was usually held in the dark, where much trickery could take place. Spiritualists grew to hate Houdini, and part of his show soon included explanations for the ways spiritualists fooled people into believing that there were ghosts in the room. This was soon after the First World War, and it seemed as if everyone in America knew someone who had died. Desperate mothers and fathers, wives and siblings, longed to have one more conversation with their loved ones. Some spiritualists would slip off their shoes and would ring hidden bells under the table, or someone working with the spiritualist would disguise themselves with ghostly fabrics and appear from across the room. Houdini thought it was terrible that people were being taken advantage of, but there are many who believe that Houdini, whose own beloved mother had died years earlier, was upset about the fake spiritualists because he was hoping to find a real one who could truly put him in contact once again with his mother.

Houdini really did die on Halloween, but it happened in Detroit while on tour, not in New York as in my story (I sent Houdini and his wife home so Victor could find them there that day). On October 23, 1926, while preparing for a performance, Houdini was backstage when he was punched in the stomach by a college student who wanted to test the magician's incredible strength. Even though he was in terrible pain, Houdini didn't want to disappoint his audience. He peformed for four more shows during the next three days before he finally collapsed backstage, and was taken to the hospital. As he lay dying, Houdini whispered to his wife, "Rosabelle, believe." "Rosabelle" had been a song she sang when she was a showgirl many years earlier. After his death, when she was to try to contact Houdini, this was the code she was to wait for. If a spiritualist said to her, "Rosabelle, believe," then Mrs. Houdini would know it really was her husband coming back from beyond the grave to talk with her. If anyone could escape death, it was Houdini.

His wife held séances each year on the anniversary of the magician's death, but after ten years, Mrs. Houdini decided he wasn't coming, and blew out the candles. She never tried again.

To this day, people remember and celebrate Houdini. His name is invoked whenever someone miraculously escapes from any situation. Politicians and babies and pets have all been compared to Houdini. And every year magicians gather at Houdini's grave at 1:26 p.m. on Halloween—the exact time and date of his death. They say the Kaddish, the Jewish prayer for the dead, and talk about his accomplishments. Reporters and photographers are always there to cover the event, and sometimes guests bearing flowers attend as well. During the ceremony a magic wand is brandished, and then broken in half, to honor the memory of Houdini, the greatest magician who ever lived.

CREATING *THE HOUDINI BOX*

⟨⟩

The Houdini Box, which was my first published book, started life as a class project while I was attending the Rhode Island School of Design. One week we had an assignment to do "something about Houdini." I was very excited about this assignment, because when I was a kid, Houdini was my hero. I loved reading books and seeing movies about Houdini. He could escape from anything, and his work exposing fake spiritualists fascinated me. I loved how strange and mysterious he was, and I found all the circumstances around his death endlessly interesting.

There were no limits on what we could do for the assignment. Some people made sculptures, some people did paintings, but I wanted to do something different. My first idea was to try to make a miniature Houdini who could disappear inside a tiny trunk, but that didn't work out—Magic, even on a scale this small, was very difficult for me! So I ended up creating a

Front view

series of glass panels that folded back and forth, accordian style, like one of those paper fans you make when it's hot outside. Each piece of glass had a different part of a picture on it, and when you looked through the front panel, all the pieces of the picture lined up and made a three-dimensional image of Houdini onstage, escaping from the Chinese Water Torture Cell, one of his most famous escapes.

I was so inspired by this project that I decided to do something a little extra, so I wrote a story about a boy who gets to meet Houdini. I would have loved to meet Houdini myself, but he died in 1926, and I wasn't born until forty years later. The great thing about writing stories, though, is you can make anything that you want happen. So I created a boy named Victor, who gets to meet his hero, Harry Houdini, and I wrote it on the back of the panels of glass. We only had seven days to make this entire project.

I handed in my project and got a pretty good grade—I think. Then I put the project away in a closet and forgot about it for many years.

After I graduated college I became very interested in making children's books. I began working at Eeyore's Books for Children in New York City. My boss, Steve Geck, seemed to know everything there was to know about children's books. He took me under his wing and sent me home every night with bags of books. This was how I learned all about children's literature. I soon felt ready to start making my own books, and that's when I remembered Victor.

Side view

Open view

RESEARCHING
THE HOUDINI BOX

When I wrote the story for my school project, I based it on what I remembered from my childhood. Those memories were enough for me to work from in college. But when I began to rewrite the story as a children's book, there were many details that I wanted to get just right, and many places where I wanted to expand the story, so I knew I would need to do a lot of research.

I started at my local library in East Brunswick, New Jersey. There, I discovered an amazing book called *The Original Houdini Scrapbook* by Walter B. Gibson (himself a magician).

Can you spot the boy who became Victor?

This book was filled with incredible pictures from Houdini's life and career, including the one reproduced here on the opposite page of Houdini doing magic for kids. I saw the boy in the center and decided that I wanted Victor to look just like that child. I think you can see the resemblance if you look at the cover of the book again.

I also started reading some biographies of Houdini, and it was in these books that I discovered Houdini would walk through brick walls onstage. This inspired the scene in *The Houdini Box*, where Victor tries to walk through the walls of his aunt Harriet's house. My next stop was the New York Public Library for the Performing Arts, where I was told I'd be able to find some files with clippings about Houdini. I remember spending a wonderful afternoon there, carefully going through original programs, newspaper clippings, and photographs from Houdini's life, and this was where I found the article that told me the Houdini Box might possibly being real (see "An Interesting Note"). This article also told me where Houdini was buried—in the Machpelah Cemetery in Queens, New York. I jumped up, found a pay phone, called information, and got in touch with someone at the cemetery, who gave me directions, so I could visit for myself. In my book, I knew there was going to be a scene at Houdini's grave, so I was eager to go and take my own pictures of the place where Houdini is buried.

I took the subway to the Cypress Hills stop, and soon found myself standing at Houdini's grave. Houdini designed the grave himself, complete with a sculpture of his own head at the center of the great monument. But to my surprise, the head was missing when I arrived at the grave. It turns out that over the years, the sculpture of Houdini's head has been stolen again and again. It seems even the sculpture of Houdini's head, like Houdini himself, is forever trying to escape.

EARLY SKETCHES

Above: When we first see Houdini onstage, I placed a sign next to him that would tell us a little more about him. But I decided that the drawing didn't need any words at all. We should just focus on Houdini himself.

Left: Before I did much research, I only had one photo of Houdini's family, and they were standing on his grave. I didn't know which woman was Houdini's wife, so I picked this one. But later I found out that his wife was a different woman, so when you see the final drawing in the book, it shows the real Mrs. Houdini.

Left: This is how I first imagined Victor up in his attic with Houdini's box. Now go back and look at the final version of the drawing. Can you see all the changes? Look at the box in both drawings. What's different? Why do you think I made that change?

Below: After I finish each drawing, I tape it up to my wall so I can see how they all look together. I'm almost done!

MAGIC TRICKS

I was a very bad magician when I was a kid. I owned several books about magic, but could not do any of the tricks. There was one trick that taught you how to balance a glass of milk on a playing card, but that just turned out to be a mess.

But there were some tricks I could do pretty well, because they were especially easy. One was called the "Ball and Vase," which you'd have to get at a magic shop. You can make a black ball appear and disappear out of a shiny red vase with a little lid. And then there's a trick I love, which requires no special effects or store-bought props at all. I like to call it "Look, Ma, My Thumb Was Cut in Half!" Here is a diagram of the trick if you would like to try it at home. If you scream while you do this trick, it helps with the illusion, and it also freaks people out.

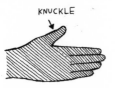

KNUCKLE

LEFT HAND IN MIRROR

RIGHT HAND IN MIRROR

TUCK THUMB DOWN INTO PALM
SO KNUCKLE STICKS UP

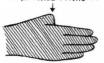

SEE TIP
OF THUMB

BEND THUMB INTO PALM.
COVER MOST OF THUMB WITH
TWO FINGERS LEAVING TIP OF
THUMB EXPOSED.

NOW BRING HANDS TOGETHER
SO FINGERS COVER MIDDLE OF
BOTH THUMBS.

NOTE HOW THE TIP OF THE RIGHT
THUMB LOOKS LIKE IT'S PART OF
THE LEFT THUMB!

SLOWLY SLIDE HANDS
APART. THIS IS WHERE
YOU SHOULD SCREAM.

BRING HANDS
BACK TOGETHER.

THE SIGN

When I first visited Houdini's grave, I was a little nervous. As I said earlier, Houdini had always been a hero of mine. I felt very connected to him. I wanted to feel this connection when I was at the grave. Since I couldn't meet Houdini in person, like Victor, I knew that this would be as close as I could get to him. I also wanted to feel that somehow, he approved of *me*.

I photographed the whole of Houdini's grave, and just as I was getting ready to leave, I found myself thinking, *I have loved Houdini almost my entire life. . . . I know his wife hadn't been able to contact him from beyond the dead, but I would like to get some kind of sign from him.* And just as I had that thought, I felt something hard underneath my foot. I bent over and brushed

Houdini's grave. Can you spot where the sculpture of Houdini's head is supposed to be?

the dirt away and found . . . a sign! I mean, an actual small brass sign, a little plaque with one word on it. All it said was CARE. I pulled the plaque out of the dirt. On the back was a long spike that was meant to keep it in the ground.

I thought about stealing it.

No one was around. Who would see me? But I knew I couldn't steal something from Houdini's grave. I put it back in the ground where I had found it.

"Care."

I loved how simple and direct it was. It was like a command. Isn't that exactly the way Houdini would say it? The word seemed to be filled with magic, as if Houdini, in his wisdom, had taken something as simple as this small word and filled it with importance and mystery. And what an important lesson it seemed to teach: Shouldn't we all care about what we are doing? Shouldn't we treat the people in our lives with care? I cared deeply about Houdini. . . . Did this mean he cared about me too? I had shivers up and down my back as I thought about all this. Later, after doing some investigating, I discovered that when someone purchases a plot in a cemetery, they can also buy something called "perpetual care," when money is paid to the groundskeepers to always mow the lawn and trim the hedges— to care for the grave. The marker I found was a reminder for the groundskeeper that someone had bought perpetual care for Houdini's grave.

But the fact is the little sign had been hidden, buried in the dirt, and I found it beneath my foot at the exact moment I was hoping to find a sign from Houdini! Was it a coincidence? Maybe. But I think that this little sign might, indeed, have been a sign from Houdini, and if it was, I think the message is worth remembering . . .

FOR FURTHER READING

Fleischman, Sid. *Escape! The Story of the Great Houdini.* New York: Greenwillow Books, 2006. Sid Fleischman is a brilliant writer, and a magician as well, and he knew Mrs. Houdini personally!

Lutes, Jason, and Nick Bertozzi. *Houdini: The Handcuff King.* New York: Hyperion, 2008. This is a wonderful graphic novel that shows how Houdini performed one of his famous escapes, and focuses on his relationship with his wife.

Mullin, Rita Thievon. *Harry Houdini: Death-Defying Showman.* New York: Sterling, 2007. A biography of the great magician for young people, packed with amazing photos and posters, as well as a handy time line of Houdini's life.

Silverman, Kenneth. *Houdini!!! The Career of Ehrich Weiss: American Self-Liberator, Europe's Eclipsing Sensation, World's Handcuff King and Prison Breaker.* New York: HarperCollins Publishers, 1996. For older kids and adults, this is the most authoritative biography there is about the great magician.

www.houdinitribute.com/links.html This website has lots of great information about Houdini, recordings of his voice, and links to other websites about him. You won't be disappointed.